For Joey and Juno

First published 2019 by Walker Books Ltd
87 Vauxhall Walk, London SE11 5HJ

10 9 8 7 6 5 4 3 2 1

© 2019 Chris Judge

The right of Chris Judge to be identified as author and illustrator of
this work has been asserted by him in accordance with the Copyright,
Designs and Patents Act 1988

This book has been typeset in Bauer Grotesk OT

Printed in China

British Library Cataloguing in Publication
Data: a catalogue record for this book is
available from the British Library

ISBN 978-1-4063-7092-8

www.walker.co.uk

TINY and TEENY

Chris Judge

WALKER BOOKS
AND SUBSIDIARIES

LONDON · BOSTON · SYDNEY · AUCKLAND

Deep down
in between the blades of grass,
in a shiny red apple,
in a little-bitty
snug of a place ...
lived Tiny and Teeny.

Can
you
see
them?

Keep looking...

Keep looking...

Closer still ...
close ONE eye ...
squint a bit...

There you go!

That's Tiny,
that's her house,
and that's her pet,
Teeny.

Their home was right on the edge of Glengadget! A busy, buzzing place. And no one was busier and buzzier than Tiny herself, who loved to be out and about, helping others wherever she could.

What was she up to
this week?

On Monday, Tiny helped Mandy Small in her garden.

Tiny was pretty handy with a lawnmower.

On Tuesday, Bitsy Jones called round and Tiny read to her.
Bitsy loved when Tiny did all the funny voices.

On Wednesday, Tiny took Minikin's twins
for a stroll through town.

The twins were *quite*
a handful.

On Thursday, Tiny helped Minnie with her shopping.
Minnie liked green beans. LOTS of them.

PETIT POIS GREENGROCER

Peanuts
3 for 2

By Friday night, well, Tiny was exhausted.
So, she sat out in her garden with Teeny and,
together, they looked at the stars.

And soon, without even knowing it, Tiny fell fast asleep, dreaming of flying through space past green beans and glittering shooting stars...

Oh no! Oh *dear!*

What has happened to Tiny and Teeny's beautiful home?

Boutique

MUS

Joey

Cof

HOU

Police Chief Yeabig had never seen anything like it.

Doctor Scopic shook her head very seriously.

It was 'metamorphic', she said.

There wasn't anything anyone could do.

Tiny knew this to be true.

Their home was ... squashed.

Tiny and Teeny were given a room in *The Grand Hotel.* But it wasn't their little red apple house, it wasn't home.

Tiny felt lost.

Where would their home be now?

Tiny's friends wanted to help.
So, on Monday, Mandy Small gave
Tiny a picnic in her garden.

On Tuesday, Bitsy McGee took Tiny to the library and they read together.

On Wednesday, Minnie took Tiny shopping for new clothes.

On Thursday, Minikin and her twins took Tiny to the park.

And, on Friday ... something BIG happened in Glengadget...

Oh, wow-wee! Oh, GOSH!
Tiny couldn't believe her eyes!

A new house for Tiny and Teeny!
Made for them, by all their friends.

Deep down, in between the blades of grass,
in a little-bitty snug of a place,
right on the edge of Glengadget,
Tiny and Teeny lived together in their
stripy green watermelon home.

Can you see them?

Wave hello.

Boutique